CHEETAHS
World's Fastest Cats

Amelie von Zumbusch

PowerKiDS
press

New York

Published in 2007 by The Rosen Publishing Group, Inc.
29 East 21st Street, New York, NY 10010

First Edition

Book Design: Erica Clendening
Layout Design: Julio Gil

Photo Credits: Cover, pp. 1, 6, 16, 18, 20 © www.shutterstock.com; pp. 4, 10 © Digital Vision; p. 8 © www.istockphoto.com/Jurie Maree; p. 12 © Digital Stock; p. 14 © www.istockphoto.com/andydidyk.

Library of Congress Cataloging-in-Publication Data

Zumbusch, Amelie von.
  Cheetahs : world's fastest cats / Amelie von Zumbusch. — 1st ed.
     p. cm. — (Dangerous cats)
  Includes bibliographical references and index.
  ISBN-13: 978-1-4042-3630-1 (library binding)
  ISBN-10: 1-4042-3630-9 (library binding)
  1. Cheetah—Juvenile literature. I. Title.
  QL737.C23Z793 2007
  599.75'9—dc22
                                                    2006019575

Manufactured in the United States of America

Contents

4

The Cheetah

The cheetah is a large, spotted cat. Cheetahs are the fastest members of the cat family. In fact cheetahs are the fastest land animals on Earth. There are birds that can fly faster than a cheetah can run. However, there are no animals that can run more quickly than a cheetah can.

The name "cheetah" comes from a Hindi word that means "spotted one." Hindi is one of the languages spoken in India.

Cheetahs can purr, just as house cats do. However, they cannot roar, as lions and tigers do.

What Cheetahs Look Like

Cheetahs have small heads. They have long, thin bodies. A cheetah's **spine** bends easily. Its **flexible** back lets a cheetah take very long **strides** while it is running. A running cheetah can spring more than 20 feet (6 m) in one stride.

Cheetahs have strong, thin legs. They have sharp claws on their feet. A cheetah's claws dig into the ground. They keep the cheetah from tripping when it runs.

A cheetah's tail is between 26 and 33 inches (66–84 cm) long.

King Cheetahs

Cheetahs most often have a tan coat with black spots. A cheetah's spots are round or oval. Cheetahs have a black line on either side of their nose. These lines are called tear stripes.

Some cheetahs have spots that run together to make stripes. These cheetahs are called king cheetahs. **Scientists** used to think that spotted cheetahs and king cheetahs were different **species**. They now know that they are members of the same species.

King cheetahs are not common. Most cheetahs have spots.

Cheetahs are **carnivores**. They hunt other animals for food. **Gazelles** are the cheetah's favorite food. However, cheetahs also eat **antelopes**, wild pigs, rabbits, and other animals.

Cheetahs creep up to their **prey**. When a cheetah gets quite close to the animal it is hunting, it breaks into a run. The cheetah uses its long front legs to trip its prey. Cheetahs kill their prey by biting its throat.

Cheetahs generally hunt early in the morning or late in the afternoon.

The Fastest Animal on Earth

A cheetah can run 70 miles per hour (113 km/h)! This is about the same speed that a fast car on a highway moves. However, a cheetah cannot run this fast for very long. After a few hundred yards (m), the cheetah gets too hot and tired to run any longer.

Cheetahs must eat their prey quickly. This is because other animals, such as lions, often steal a cheetah's prey.

A cheetah can run about three times faster than the fastest person in the world.

14

Where Cheetahs Live

Cheetahs live on mostly open land, such as **plains** or grasslands. It is hard to see a cheetah's spotted, tan coat in the grass. This helps the cheetah creep up on its prey when it hunts.

Most cheetahs live on the **savannahs** of Africa. There are also a small number of cheetahs that live in Iran. Cheetahs once lived in India and Pakistan, but there are few or no cheetahs there today.

This cheetah lives on the plains of the Masai Mara park in Kenya.

Baby Cheetahs

Baby cheetahs are covered with a **mantle** of long, gray fur. They begin to lose this mantle when they are about four months old.

Mother cheetahs have to hunt for food almost every day. While they are out hunting, mother cheetahs hide their babies in the grass. Mother cheetahs carry their babies to a new hiding place every few days. This makes it harder for **predators** to find the babies.

Its furry mantle makes this baby cheetah hard to see in the grass.

18

Growing Up

When they are about six months old, young cheetahs start to follow their mother when she goes hunting. They learn how to hunt and care for themselves by watching her.

Young cheetahs leave their mother when they are between one and two years old. They stay together for a few more months. Then the cheetah sisters go off to live on their own. Cheetah brothers often stay together for the rest of their lives.

This mother cheetah and her baby are looking for prey. Cheetah mothers teach their children which animals to hunt.

Cheetahs and People

Cheetahs almost never **attack** people. In the past many powerful people have had pet cheetahs. Akbar the Great, who ruled India in the 1500s, was said to have owned 9,000 cheetahs. However, people are no longer allowed to keep cheetahs as pets. This is because cheetahs have become **endangered** animals.

Though cheetahs do not often attack people, they are still strong, wild animals. People should always be very careful around cheetahs.

This cheetah is snarling. When a cheetah snarls at you, it is telling you to stay away.

Endangered Cheetahs

Cheetahs are endangered animals. Hunters kill cheetahs for their beautiful coats. Farmers kill cheetahs because they fear that the big cats will kill their farm animals. Farmers also take over the land where cheetahs live to build farms. This leaves the cheetahs with no place to live or hunt.

Luckily some people have set aside land for wildlife parks. Wildlife parks are large pieces of land where wild animals, like cheetahs, can live safely.

Glossary

antelopes (AN-teh-lohps) Thin, fast animals found in Asia and Africa.

attack (uh-TAK) To start a fight with.

carnivores (KAR-nih-vorz) Animals that eat other animals.

endangered (in-DAYN-jerd) Describing a kind of animal that has almost died out.

flexible (FLEK-sih-bul) Moving and bending in many ways.

gazelles (ga-ZELZ) Small, deerlike animals from Africa and Asia.

mantle (MAN-tul) Fur above an animal's coat.

plains (PLAYNZ) A place with mostly flat lands that have few or no trees.

predators (PREH-duh-terz) Animals that kill other animals for food.

prey (PRAY) An animal that is hunted by another animal for food.

savannahs (suh-VA-nuhz) Grasslands with few trees or bushes.

scientists (SY-un-tists) People who study the world.

species (SPEE-sheez) A single kind of living thing. All people are one species.

spine (SPYN) The bones that run down an animal's back.

strides (STRYDZ) Long steps.

Index

A

antelopes, 11

B

birds, 5

C

carnivores, 11

G

gazelles, 11
grasslands, 15

H

heads, 7
Hindi, 5

I

India, 5, 15, 21

L

legs, 7, 11

M

mantle, 17

P

people, 21–22
plains, 15
predators, 17
prey, 11, 13, 15

S

savannahs, 15
scientists, 9
species, 9
spine, 7
stride(s), 7

Web Sites

Due to the changing nature of Internet links, PowerKids Press has developed an online list of Web sites related to this book. This site is updated regularly. Please use this link to access the list:
www.powerkidslinks.com/dcats/cheetahs/